WHAT YOU DON'T KNOW

WHAT YOU DON'T KNOW

A Story of Liberated Childhood

By Anastasia Higginbotham

dottir press

Published in 2021 by Dottir Press
33 Fifth Avenue
New York, NY 10003

Dottirpress.com

FIRST EDITION

Third printing: OCTOBER 2021

Illustrations and text by Anastasia Higginbotham
Photography by Alexa Hoyer
Production by Drew Stevens and Frances Ross

Trade distribution by Consortium Book Sales and Distribution, www.cbsd.com.

Library of Congress Cataloging-in-Publication Data is available for this title.
ISBN 978-1-9483-4029-8

PRINTED IN THE UNITED STATES OF AMERICA BY WORZALLA

For Abraham, whose 1980s
childhood in a small,
homophobic town radicalized me
&
for Moxie, who is real and
free—right now, today.

"I don't need tolerance, I don't need acceptance. What we demand is your respect for our humanity."

—Billy Porter

Billy Porter by
Noor Buckles-Souirgi,
Class of 2020,
The Churchill School, NYC

What you don't Know
is that life was great
before Kindergarten.

I invented stories and characters
that thrilled my mother.
I painted my face.
I danced.

It was fun, and I was free.

Then school happened.

School is scary.
Nice flower jacket, f*****!

And scared people
are not the most
generous, or Kind.

Did I say scared?
I mean scarred.
I mean both.

Stop flouncing around and giggling with the girls, Demetrius!

I'm putting you on the red!

Now that I'm in
middle school,
I have to wonder . . .

. . . what are we even learning here
besides all the things we have to be
afraid of and
all of the things
we can't do?

I can't fail these tests.
I can't fail to protect these Kids.

116
FACULTY
Is anyone safe
to be genuine,
to be whole,
to be real?
I can't pay my bills.

Thank God, I have friends here.
Guardians.
Protectors.
Family, in a way.

I have an idea for us! Talk to me after school!
MOXIE
(my friend, who's queer like me)

ADDIE
(the radical
librarian)
If I don't have
what you need,
I'll find it.

I see you.
MIZZOH
(my teacher who loves me)

I'm here.
MR. VÁSQUEZ
(our counselor,
who's also queer)

But even they are a little bit scared.

How do I Know?

I sense it—one of the benefits
of being "sensitive."

They let me Know about
safe spaces . . .

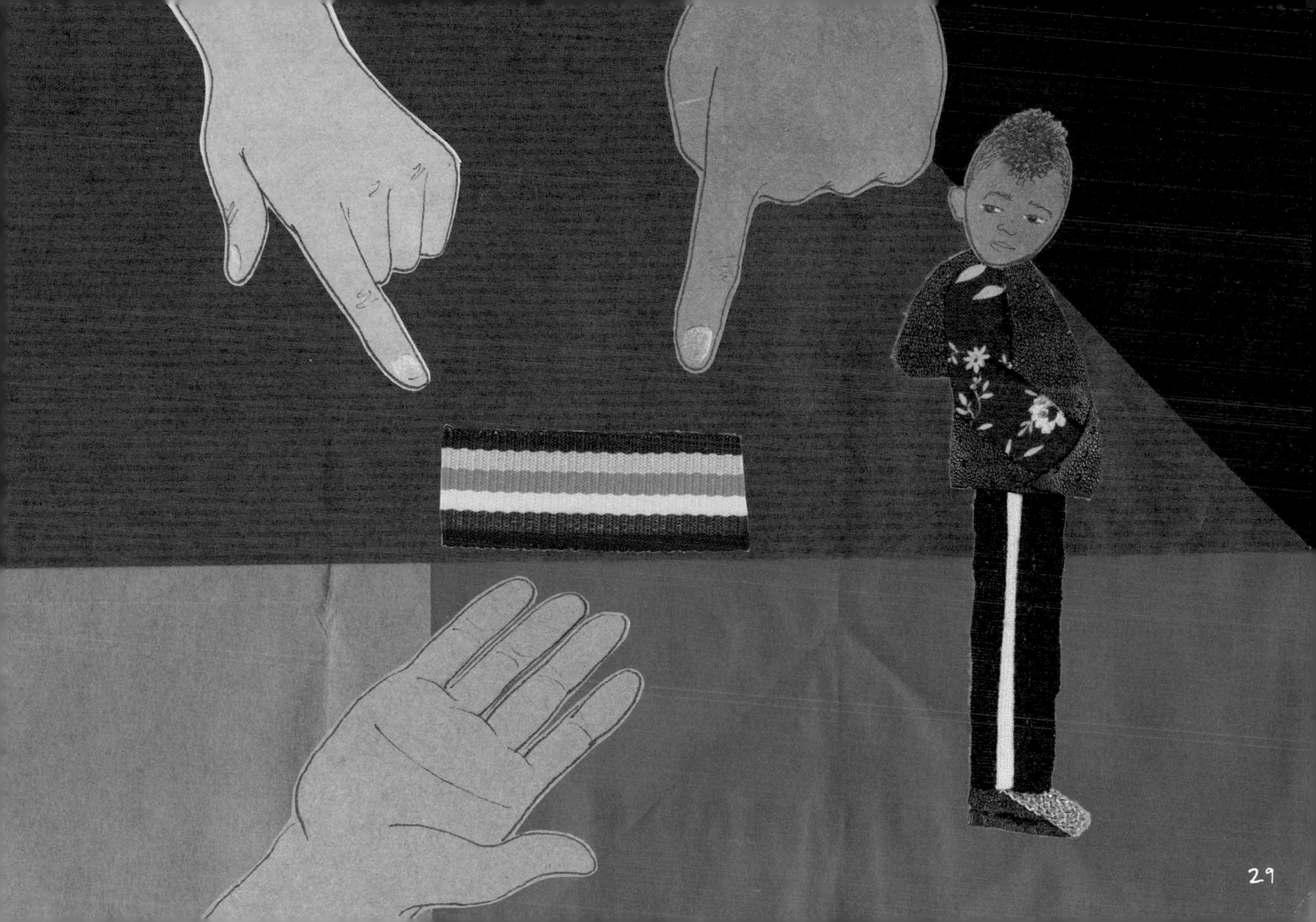

. . . which means they Know
I could be in danger.
I'm glad we agree on that.

We're starting a podcast. We're gonna tell our stories.
Who is we?
Us, the ones who are in this together.
Who are we telling?
Everyone who listens.

What you don't Know is there are lots of people I have to hide myself from—but my dad is not one of them.

He has always seen me true.

He gives me space
to be who I am.
I do the same
for him.
The air is easy
between us.
There's enough.

He teaches me what his dad taught him.
Don't let anybody out there tell you who you are.

All you need to be is you.

My father loves me
completely.
And you bet I feel it.

See you Sunday!

My mother
fights for us.

She was a sensitive Kid, too.

The world is so ****ing unfair!

She's got her own sense of justice and her own ideas about God.

It may sound strange, but when she's cussing at her phone, I feel loved and seen.

The news is **atrocious.** Hide my phone for me?
OCTAVIA E. BUTLER
Parable of

She lets me Know that I matter and that I'm not the one with the problem.

What you don't know is even though I'm loved at home, the world's ugliness toward gay people lands *right ON me.* They make laws against us, call us evil, try to convert us!

And what about the ones who *aren't* loved at home? What about the kids whose own families reject them?

"God is Change.
Shape God."
—Octavia E. Butler
OCTAVIA

Churches can preach all they want about love—the only thing that I feel when I'm here is shame.

48

But the shame isn't mine and it's not coming from "God." I have nothing to be ashamed of.

My spirit floats free.

Jesus!
Yes!

You're here!
Always and everywhere.

Do you Know what's happening down there?
Yes.

Does it hurt your feelings if I don't believe in you?
It's my job to believe in you, and I do.

So we're cool?
Always.

Hey, Jesus?
Are there other gods besides you?
Hey what?

Divinity is everywhere, in everyone and everything.

EXIT

Are you gonna punish the people of Earth who hate me and blame it on you?
Nope. Everyone is invited to love and be loved.

How about him?
Especially him. Love the dress, Billy!
Yours, too, baby!

Even— ?

Yes.

Wanna Know what I love, Jesus?
Always.
I love that you and me are Black.

EXCUSE ME—
I don't mean to be *rude*, but you need to keep your son awake in church and teach him *right* from *wrong*.
There's a place for people like that and it's not heaven! And stop dressing him in flowers— he's a BOY.
?!

What you don't Know is . . .

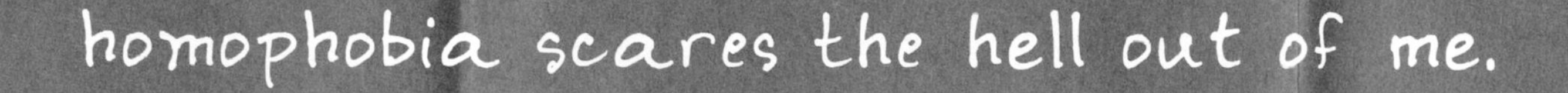
homophobia scares the hell out of me.

Well, what you
just said is very rude.
Mind your own business
and stay out
of ours.

Tell me again why we still come here?
I like the smell of the incense. I'm so sorry that happened.

Maybe someday
I'll understand the hurt
that causes the fear
that causes the hate
that causes the violence
and stupidity.

I said, *maybe.*

But LOVE, I Know all about.

Thanks for telling me. That sounds awful.
I'm sorry he had to experience that.
I am too. Are you really gonna stop going, just like that?
Yes. I know how to find God. I don't need a building.

Love you, Mom.
And . . . thanks.

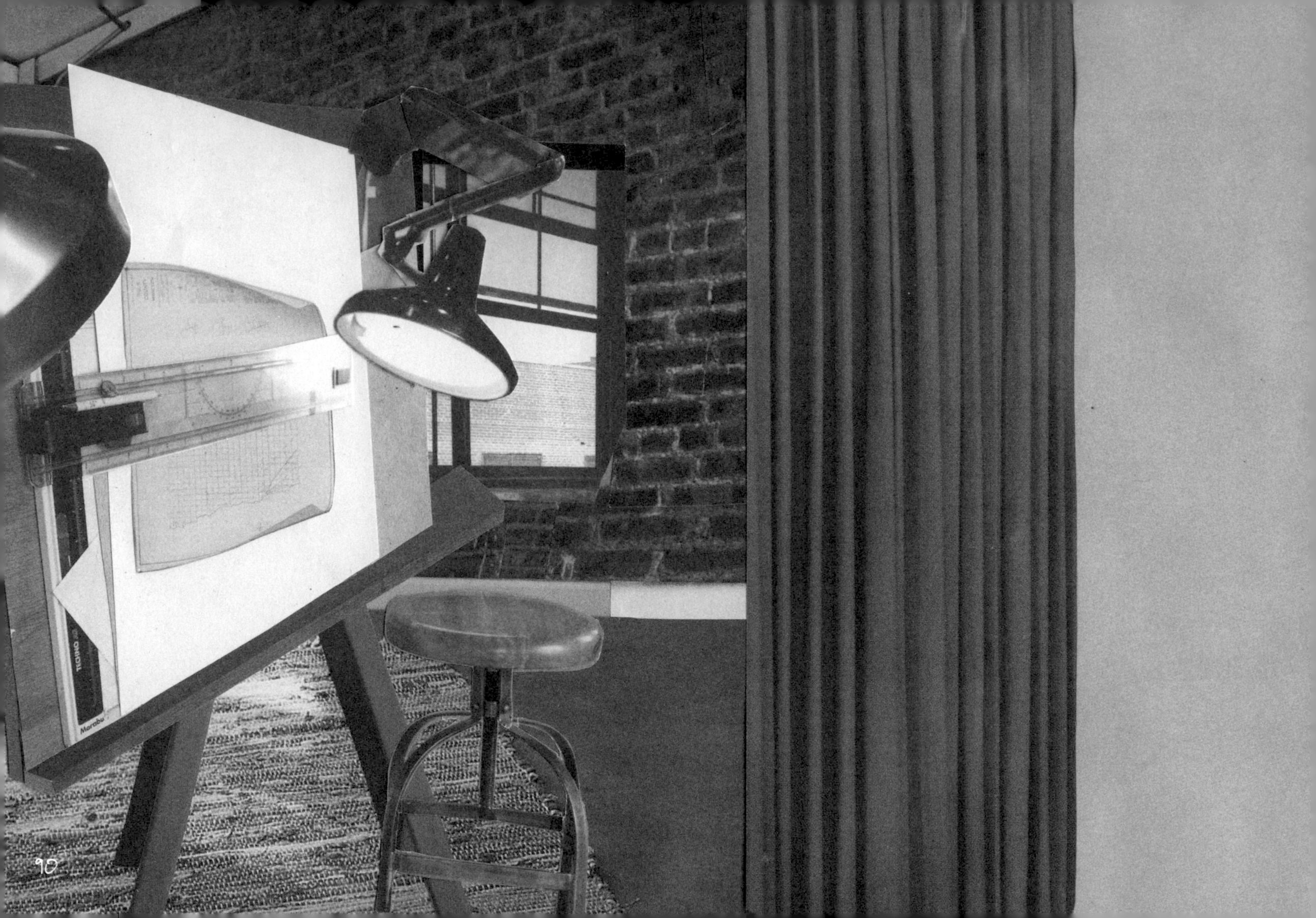
Marabu

Your aunt Viv's coming over.
Can Moxie come too? We're recording our podcast.
Absolutely.

Before we were called Black,
white, brown, queer . . .
Before the world saw our bodies
and decided we were
a boy or a girl
or dark
or light . . .
our
bodies
learned
Earth
Outer
space
nature
constant
change
stand
back
behold
us
GOD
imagine
you

Before we learned about our sensitivities,
disabilities, test scores, zip codes . . .

Before and beyond our being
your child or that child . . .
a child of this nation or that one . . .
a child of one god or many . . .
a child of earth or outer space . . .

. . . we were our own true nature.

The Kids are making a podcast in D's room.

OKaaay!
Kitche
Table

We are born in a constant state of change
and stay changing.

Can you stand to stand back and behold us,
let us be?

All that we are
and all that you are not.
God! Imagine that!
COMPOSITION BOOK
Moxie and Q's Podcast
our
bodies
learned
Earth
Outer
space
nature
constant
change
stand
back
behold
us

When the world is the way it should be, the way it can be . . .
Kitchen Table

the way it will be because it has to be . . .
. . . in that world, people's imaginations will be bigger.

Beauty will shine out of us like starlight.

Tony Award-winning
Actor Billy Porter

We will rewrite the rules we live by
and love the world into balance.

U.S. Representatives Rashida Tlaib, Ayanna Pressley,
Ilhan Omar, and Alexandria Ocasio-Cortez

Sensitivity will be valued
as the superpower it is.

And we'll all be seen

and celebrated

and safe to be genuine,

to be whole,

to be real.

It's live, D! I sent you the link!

We're celebrating our new podcast at the skating rink this Friday. Come if you can!

Sweetie, I was already gonna be at the rink this Friday, and I would love to celebrate with you.
116
FACULTY

What you don't Know is I'm always gonna
love myself and find others who do, too.
I'll wear clothes so shiny you'll see your
own fears—
and flowers to remind you my life force
breaKs concrete.
I'll claim every color in the rainbow as armor
and glow even brighter in the dark.

How do I look, Ma?

You look like YOU.
You thrill me,
Demetrius.

When the world is the way it should be—the way it can be—the way it will be because it has to be—in *that* world, people's imaginations will be bigger.

All of me is all I want to be. And love is all I'm about.
I'm Moxie—
—and I'm D.
Thanks for listening. We. Are. Out.

You've got
a great voice, D.
Keep it comin'.

Imagine how easy it could be
if love were no trouble . . .

. . . no trouble at all.

What I Know is that

LOVE is the easiest part.

I feel it.

I get it.

I give it.

I am it.

Get used to it.

Love, thanks, and credit to:

Jesse Dorris, Darryl Gibson, Drew Stevens, and Benny Vásquez, who spoke with me about surviving childhood, boyhood, family and church; about racism, sex, God and identity; and about the importance of having girls as friends.

Noor Buckles-Souirgi, who drew Bayard Rustin and Audre Lorde (page 27), Billy Porter (page 7 & 105), and Representatives Rashida Tlaib, Ayanna Pressley, Ilhan Omar, and Alexandria Ocasio-Cortez (page 107)—thanks for swooping in at the end to add sparkle to the roller skaters.

Rev angel Kyodo Williams, who taught me that "love is space"; Noleca Anderson Radway, mother of Moxie, whose Raising Rebels podcast about "oppressed parents raising free children" inspired Moxie's podcast; Jill Flowers, who dared me to consider: But what if the children are safe?; and Octavia E. Butler, who envisioned our way through the future that is happening now.

My sister, Alaina Sarah, who, as a child, imagined that God looked like the Jesus in this book (actual size), and allowed me to use her design.

The beautiful people who fire my activism and consented to be drawn: Spencer Ellis (father), Wanda Olugbala (Mizzoh), Moxie Radway (Moxie), yvette shipman (Aunt Viv), Addie Smock (radical librarian), and Benny Vásquez (Mr. Vásquez). The child's white mother is me, my mother, my sisters, and many dear friends.

Larissa Melo Pienkowski, for the care you gave to the script; the team at Dottir Press—Erin, Kait, Kayla, and Jodi—for promoting me and my work; Frances Ross, for your precise editing of this book's illustrations and contribution to its final design; Drew Stevens, whose artistry and soulful collaboration has been vital to every book we've made—you are a joy; and Jennifer Baumgardner, for loving me and what I make, and for trusting me.

My partner Jon Luongo and our sons, Lionel and Sabatino, and my parents, siblings, niblings, and friends, who affirm, love, and support me in all the ways.

My brother Abraham, who helped me go the whole way into the heart of what's the matter.

Other Books by Anastasia Higginbotham

NOT MY IDEA: A Book About Whiteness

TELL ME ABOUT SEX, GRANDMA

DEATH IS STUPID

DIVORCE IS THE WORST